The Problem of the Hot World

Pam Bonsper - Dick Rink

ISBN-13: 978-1514648544
ISBN:10: 1514648547

Printed in the United States of America
First published: June 2015

Dedicated to our beautiful planet and all the plants and animals that live on it.

The deer with the big antlers knew it.
The bear with the big belly knew it.
The fox with the red tail was too foxy to admit it, but he knew it.

The mole came slowly out of his hole.
The owl flew sleepily from his tree.

And when the big yellow sun came up...
they all knew it!

Something was wrong in the forest.
Something was wrong with the trees,
with the rocks and the sky.

Leaves were not growing on the trees.
Moss was not growing on the rocks.
Rain was not falling.

The world was too hot.

"What should we do?"
shouted the deer, the bear,
and the mole.

The owl tilted his sleepy head and said, "I usually have good advice, but I am just too sleepy in the morning.

Please ask me when it's dark and perhaps I will have an answer."

"Oh, no you don't!" yapped the foxy fox.

"This is something that must be dealt with right now!

We must all unite and ask the forest fairies what we can do to help our beautiful forest."

The deer thought about it.
The bear sat down and rubbed his growling tummy.
The mole lay on his back and looked at the sky.
The fox thought he should rub the ground.

But no forest fairies appeared.

Finally the wise old owl flew in circles above them and then landed on the dry rocks.

"I think it's too hot for the fairies. Their wings have turned to dust."

"Oh, no!" cried the bear, whose belly was quickly shrinking.

"I depend upon the fairies to help the plants to make the flowers, to help the bees to make the honey.

What can we do?"

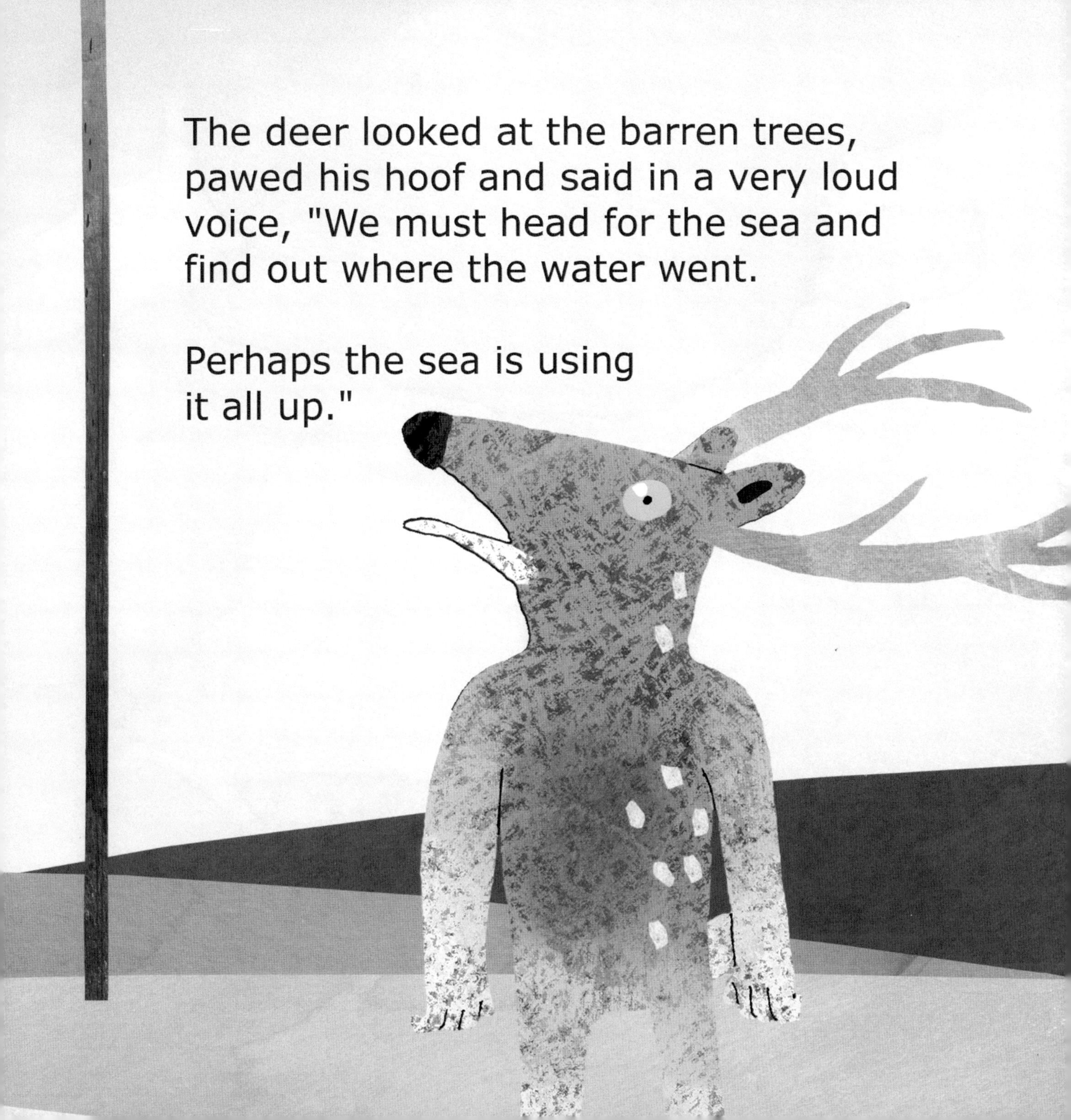

The deer looked at the barren trees, pawed his hoof and said in a very loud voice, "We must head for the sea and find out where the water went.

Perhaps the sea is using it all up."

Everyone was in agreement.

Off they went to solve the problem of the hot world.

They traveled across the land and passed very dry creeks.

There was no breeze, just sun. They were getting weak and goofy and falling down.
Even the wise old owl lay flat on the ground.

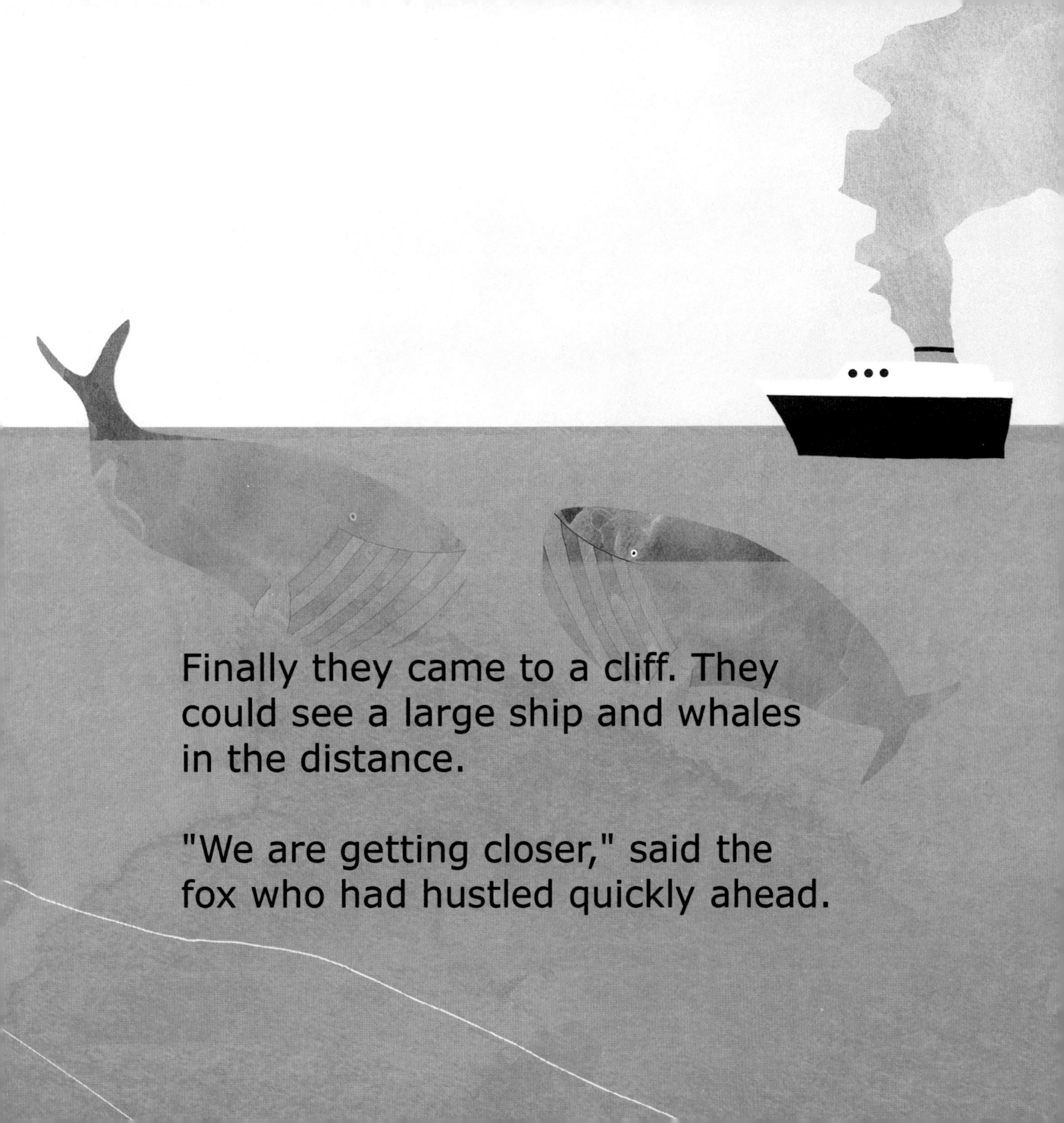

Finally they came to a cliff. They could see a large ship and whales in the distance.

"We are getting closer," said the fox who had hustled quickly ahead.

And sure enough within a short time they were seeing fish everywhere...

and water everywhere too.

The friends were so happy. They jumped and played in the cold water.

But after the bear tasted it, he flopped on the ground holding his barely there bear tummy.

"Oh, no! This is not the right water for us. What will we do?"

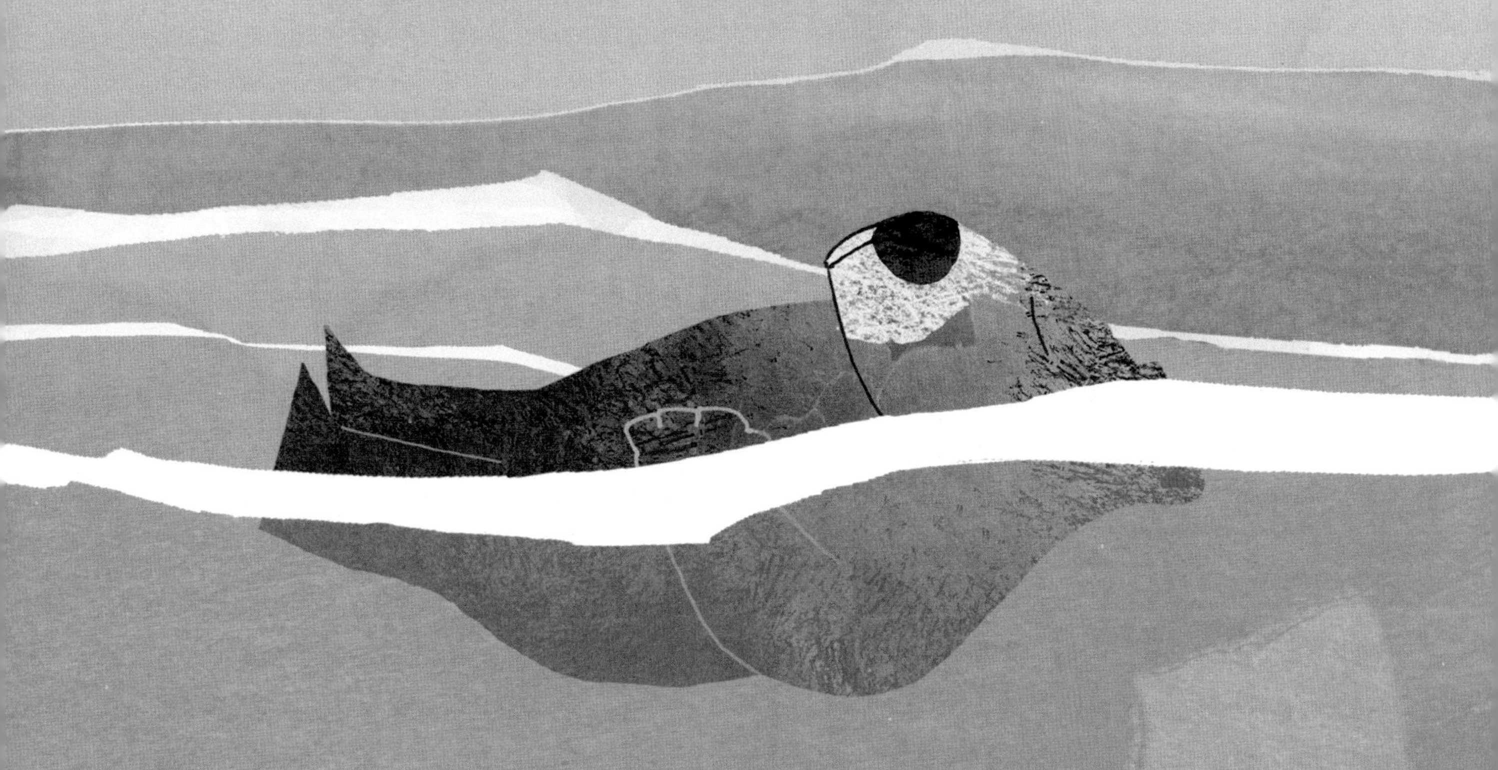

Suddenly, a baby polar bear poked his head from the icy water.

"Hey, follow me," he said. "I think I can help you guys."

"But we can't swim!" the forest friends cried.

"That's okay," said the baby polar bear.

"Just jump from one piece of ice to the next. I'll meet you at the magic cave."

The baby polar bear dove into the water and the five friends slid and flipped and jumped and zipped from one ice floe to another.

Soon there were four noses and one beak peeking through the entrance to the magic cave.

The moon began to rise and the sleepy owl clicked both his eyes wide open and said, "Whoo."

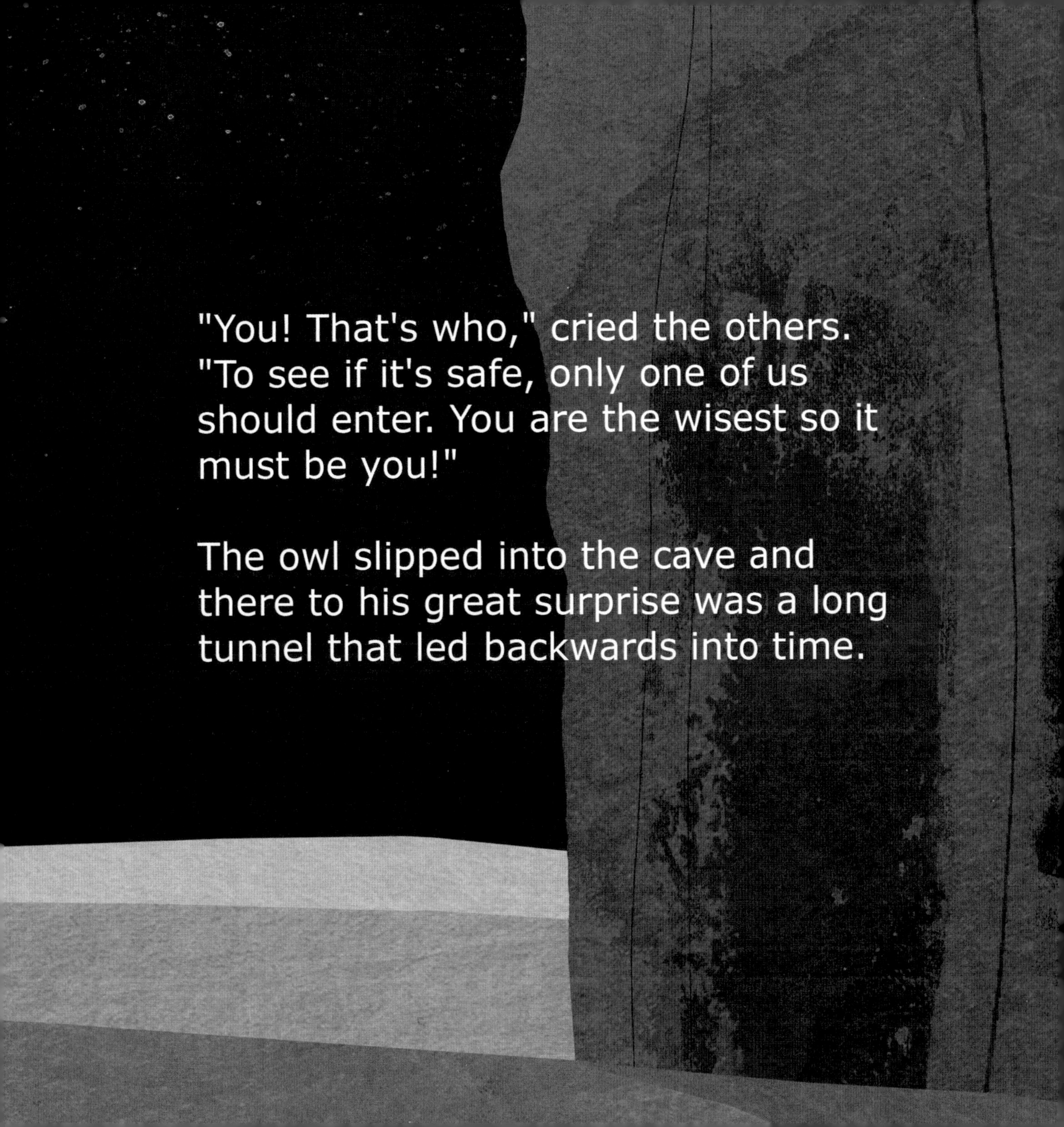

"You! That's who," cried the others. "To see if it's safe, only one of us should enter. You are the wisest so it must be you!"

The owl slipped into the cave and there to his great surprise was a long tunnel that led backwards into time.

"Come on everybody," he yelled. "Let's go through the tunnel and go back to a time when our forest was green and the plants were making flowers and the bees were making..."

He could not say another word. All of the forest friends were catapulted backwards in time.

Owl led them back to their very own woods.

Huge pine trees greeted them.

A breeze tickled their noses.

Everywhere it was green and it was not hot.

And guess what happened to the five forest friends?

Well, they all lived happily ever before.
And guess what else?

Bear got his tummy back.

Made in the USA
Middletown, DE
17 October 2020